THIS IGLOO BOOK BELONGS TO:

....

igloobooks

Published in 2019
by Igloo Books Ltd
Cottage Farm
Sywell
NN6 0BJ
www.igloobooks.com

Copyright © 2015 Igloo Books Ltd
Igloo Books is an imprint of Bonnier Books UK

1119 003
10 12 13 11 9
ISBN 978-1-78440-731-5

Written by Melanie Joyce
Illustrated by Jessika von Innerebner

Printed and manufactured in China

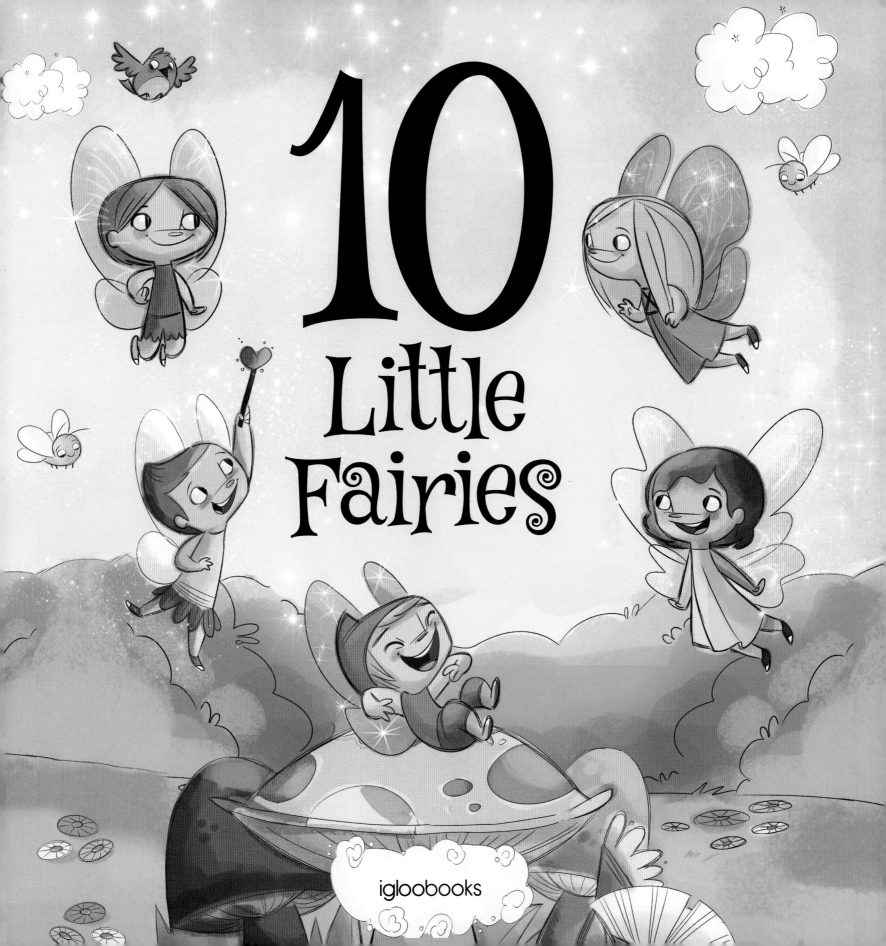

10 Little Fairies

igloobooks

In the enchanted wood, the fairy bell rings.
Ten little fairies flutter their sparkly wings.

BRRRING

"Look at the time!" they cry and flitter away.
"We're late for Fairy School today."

Ten little fairies flying in a line.

One drops her wand.

POOF!

Now there are...

Nine little fairies at the fairy gate.

SNAP! goes a dragon plant. Now there are...

Seven little fairies practising their flicks.

ATISHOO!

goes a sneezy fairy. Now there are...

Six little fairies fluttering by a hive.

BzzZZ

BzzzZZ

"Yummy!" cries a greedy fairy. Now there are...

Five little fairies by a magic door.

"What's in here?" says a nosy fairy.

Now there are...

Four little fairies come to a magic tree.

WHOOSH!

go the branches.

Now there are...

Three little fairies looking at the view.
WHOOPS! goes a clumsy fairy. Now there are...

Two little fairies, giggling, having fun.

NEIGH! goes a unicorn. Now there is...

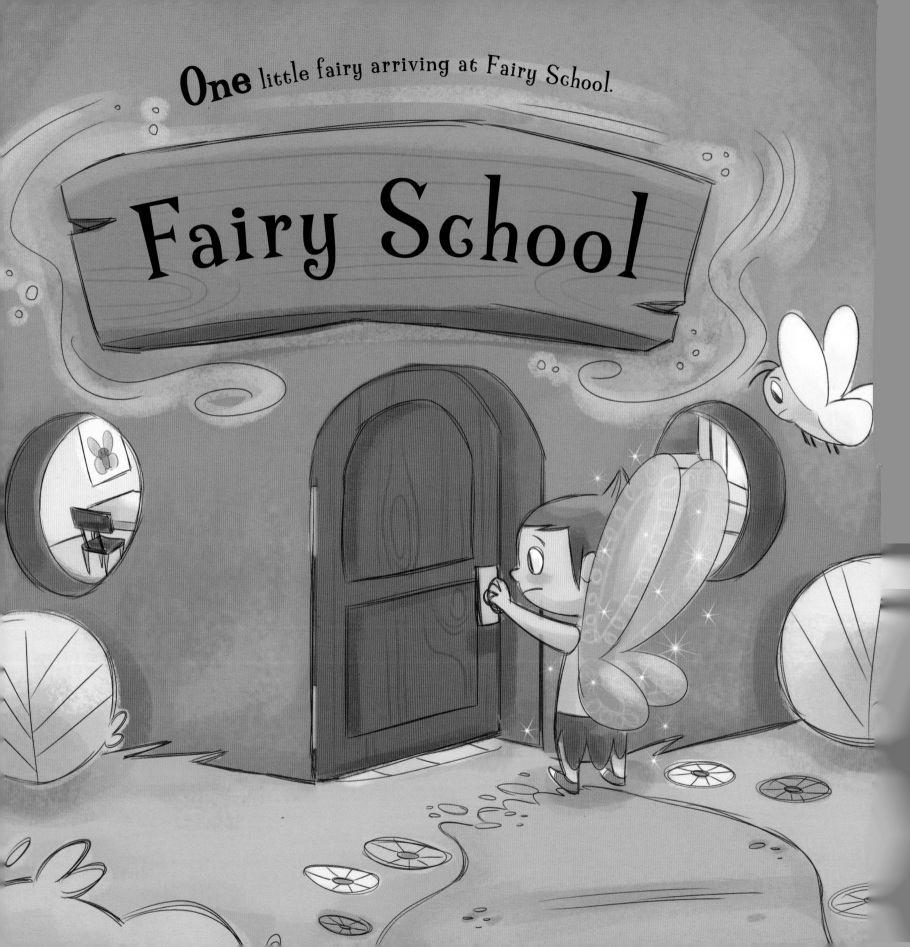

One little fairy arriving at Fairy School.

Fairy School

She's all by herself and feeling like a fool.

Miss Sparkle waves her wand and suddenly, then...

one

five

six

seven